中英雙書

喂咕嗚愛情咒

羅爾德·達爾 *Roald Dahl* ◎文
昆丁·布雷克 *Quentin Blake* ◎圖
顏銘新◎譯

Esio Trot

振聲高中
張湘君校長 強力推薦

開啟孩子創造力
由閱讀羅爾德・達爾開始

◎張湘君（振聲高中校長）

　　羅爾德・達爾（1916-1990）是一位備受矚目的英國兒童文學大師級人物。他的十九部作品，部部想像力驚人，書中創意點子令人拍案叫絕，受到廣大小讀者的喜愛，甚至還有個羅爾德・達爾日（9月13日），當天全球粉絲們紛紛舉辦各種活動，向羅爾德・達爾這位偉大的作者致敬。

　　我個人是達爾迷，他的作品不管是各種版本的作品、錄音帶或錄影帶甚至考題，我都廣泛蒐集。在國立臺北教育大學兒童英語教育研究所及亞洲大學應用外語學系教授「英美兒童文學」期間，更是將達爾的作品列入學生修課必讀書單，也不時在課堂中播放其作品改拍的電影《飛天巨桃歷險記》、《巧克力工廠的祕密》、《吹夢巨人》、《小魔女》及《女巫》，以增加學生對達爾作品不同面向的探索及體悟。

達爾創作之兒童讀物所以受人矚目，除了寫作手法高明外，主要是因為其大量運用獨特的「殘酷式幽默」，令學校老師不安，孩子的家長不悅，評論家不屑。達爾常在作品中敘述種種殘忍的場面或手段，例如把人斬成肉泥、絞成肉醬、搗爛他、砸碎他等等，這些事看在小孩子的眼裡，是有趣、誇張、惹人捧腹大笑，然而看在大人眼裡，盡是血腥恐怖、殘忍不堪，一文不值。

　　例如，《神奇魔指》書中描述一個小女孩的指頭有神奇的魔力，當她氣憤、失去控制的時候，全身會先變得很熱、很熱，右手的指尖也會開始產生帶著奔馳閃光的電流，而這電流會跳出去觸擊令她氣憤的人，他們的身上就會接二連三的發生怪事。達爾運用了「殘酷式幽默」來傳達孩子愛護動物的心聲，誇張、有趣、三不五時帶點殘忍場面的情節，非常能吸引小讀者閱讀。

　　達爾有四個孩子，每天晚上他在孩子睡覺前，也都會說故事給他們聽，因此，他的魅力不只是在文字，擅長用聲音來說故事應該也算是他的另一項特異功能。達爾常自己造字，來增加口說故事時的生動。以《大大大大的鱷魚》為例，書中有許多英文動詞鮮活傳神，如 squish、squizzle、swizzle、swoosh、Trunky 等一般字典裡查不到的「達爾專用字」，讀者可仔細推敲這些字的來源，或輕鬆略過，但不要忘了享受其中的音韻樂趣。尤其對白鮮活有趣的英文章節，可鼓勵小讀者從事英語話劇或讀者劇場的演出。

　　達爾是個喜歡搞怪的人，他搞怪的能力無遠弗屆，尤其擅長創造魔法的情節和運用幻想的元素，這可能跟達爾的母親在他和他的姊妹們孩提時代，常常說巨人等虛構人物的北歐神話故事有關。然而達爾對自己的作品要求嚴格，絕不重複使用相同的點子，往往一年才能醞釀出一個滿意的故事。

　　總之，達爾是那種只想要給孩子快樂的作家，他的作品中，孩子是絕對的王，孩子的對手（通常是大人）通常都會得到嚴厲不留情的懲罰。這些過程驚悚的反大人作品，如同《小鬼當家》一系列的電影，披露小孩其實擁有遇事沉著、冷靜、聰明、機智應對的大能力，著實讓大人驚訝！而小讀者閱讀達爾作品後，應該也能學到不管遇到多大困難，都要鎮定自若，勇敢面對，更要積極的想辦法，用自己的智慧和經驗去戰勝它！

　　紅花要有綠葉襯，三本書的插畫皆由昆丁・布萊克執筆，相得益彰。昆丁・布萊克是當代英國兒童文學界最負盛名的插畫家和作家，得過英國兒童讀物的各項大獎，他風格滑稽特異的插畫與達爾的精闢文字可謂天生一對，是無可取代的組合。

　　近年來，世界上有為的政府莫不以打造創造力國度為施政主軸，希望國家百姓能具備自我創造的意識，勇於創新、冒險與超越，以開闊的思維和自在的態度展現獨特、新奇和有趣之個人色彩，並從不斷嘗試創造的過程中發現學習樂趣。

　　達爾作品總能帶給讀者豐富的想像力、創造力及閱讀的樂趣，在此我誠摯的、歡喜的將它的新版推薦給臺灣的大小讀者。

幾年前，當我的孩子還小的時候，我們常會在花園裡養一、兩隻烏龜。在那個年代裡，經常可以看到烏龜在一些人家的草坪上或是後院裡慢慢的爬著。你可以在任何一家寵物店裡很便宜的買到牠們，而且在所有孩子的寵物之中，牠們可能是最不麻煩，也是最無害的。

烏龜過去都是幾千隻一起被裝在大貨箱裡進口到英格蘭來的，絕大多數都來自於非洲北部。不過在幾年前，通過了一條法律，禁止再輸入任何的烏龜。這並不是為了要保護我們，因為這些小烏龜並不會危害任何人。這條法律純粹是出自於對烏龜本身的善意。你們知道，進口牠們的商人，通常既不供水又不給食物的將上百隻烏龜緊緊塞進貨箱裡，在這種惡劣的狀況之下，牠們有許多都在海上的旅程中死亡。因此，政府就禁止了這整項買賣，來避免這麼殘酷的事情繼續發生。

在這個故事裡，你們讀到的所有事件，都是發生在任何人都可以隨意在一家寵物店買到一隻可愛小烏龜的日子裡。

荷畢先生
Mr Hoppy

阿肥
Alfie

喜爾福太太
Mrs Silver

寵物店老闆
Pet-shop Owner

烏龜捕手
The Tortoise-catcher

喂咕嗚愛情咒

荷畢先生住在一棟高高水泥大樓的高層小公寓裡。他一個人住，他一直很孤單。退休了之後，他變得比從前更孤單了。

荷畢先生一生中有兩件最鍾愛的事情。其一是他在陽台上所種的花花草草。他把它們種在盆子裡、桶子裡和籃子裡，當夏天來臨時，這座小陽台便充滿令人狂野迷亂的色彩。

荷畢先生第二個鍾愛的，則是只有他自己一個人知道的祕密。

荷畢先生陽台下方緊鄰著另一座陽台，那座陽台比他自己的陽台延伸出建築物外許多，因此他總是可以清楚看到下面發生了些什麼事情。那座陽台是一位叫作喜爾福太太的迷人中年婦女所擁有的。喜爾福太太也是獨居的寡婦，而且她並不曉得，其實她就是荷

喂咕嗚愛情咒

畢先生祕密愛戀著的女主角。荷畢先生已經偷偷的隔著陽台暗戀她許多年了，但他很害羞，他一直無法說服自己能向她透露一絲絲的愛意。

　　每天早晨，荷畢先生和喜爾福太太會一個朝下、一個往上，彼此禮貌性的寒暄幾句，但也僅止於此而已。他倆陽台之間的距離也許不到幾碼，但是對荷畢先生來說，卻好像相隔有百萬哩之遙。他多麼渴望邀請喜爾福太太上來喝杯茶和吃個餅乾，但是每當話到了嘴邊，他就提不起勇氣。正如我所說的，他是一個非常非常害羞的人。

喂咕嗚愛情咒

噢，如果可能的話——他不斷的告訴自己，如果可能的話，他要做一些了不起的事情，譬如拯救她的性命，或是把她從一群拿著武器的惡棍手中解救出來；如果可能的話，他要幹一番轟轟烈烈的大事業，好讓自己變成她眼裡的英雄；如果可能的話⋯⋯

問題是喜爾福太太把她所有的關愛都送給了別人，而那個別人，正是一隻叫作「阿肥」的小烏龜。每天早上，當荷畢先生從他的陽台上瞧下來，看到喜爾福太太對著阿肥溫柔低語，輕輕撫弄著牠的龜殼的

時候，他就感到莫名的嫉妒。假如每天早上，喜爾福太太輕撫的是他的殼、輕聲細語的對象是他，就算自己變成一隻烏龜，他也絲毫不在乎！

阿肥已經住在喜爾福太太家很多年了，不論寒暑都住在她的陽台上。陽台的周圍鋪有厚木條，避免阿

肥走著走著就掉出去，此外，在某個角落，還有一間小房子，好讓阿肥晚上爬進去保暖。

　　等到十一月，天氣變得比較冷了，喜爾福太太會

在阿肥的房子裡面放滿乾稻草，然後阿肥就會爬進去，

把自己深深埋進稻草裡，不吃不喝的睡上幾個月，這

就叫作「冬眠」。

　　初春時，阿肥透過牠的龜殼感覺到天氣變得暖和
了，牠就會甦醒過來，非常緩慢的從陽台上的小房子
爬出來。接著，喜爾福太太便會高興的拍著她的手大
叫：「歡迎回來，親愛的！哎喲，我好想念你啊！」

　　總在這時候，荷畢先生會格外希望他能夠和阿

肥交換位置，他希望自己乾脆變

成一隻烏龜算了。

　　這天，五月裡某個晴朗的早晨， 發生了一

件改變──甚至震撼荷畢先生一生的事。那天他

正巧倚著他的陽台欄杆，看著喜爾福太太餵阿肥

吃早餐。

　　「來吃些萵苣菜心，我的小可愛。」她說。

「還有一片新鮮的番茄和青脆的芹菜。」

「早啊，喜爾福太太，」荷畢先生說。「阿肥今天早上看起來不錯啊！」

「牠是不是很棒！」喜爾福太太往上瞧，並且盯著他說。

「絕對是很棒。」荷畢先生昧著良心說。正當他往下瞧見喜爾福太太的笑臉朝上迎視他時，那想了一千遍的想法又跑了出來：她怎會如此的漂亮，如此的甜美、溫柔、善良，他的心被愛情刺痛著。

「我真希望牠能夠長得快一點兒，」喜爾福太太繼續說。「每年春天，當牠從冬眠中醒來的時候，我會用廚房裡的秤子秤牠。你知道嗎？我養了牠足足十一年了，牠卻長大不到三盎司！幾乎沒有長大！」

「牠現在有多重呢？」荷畢先生問她。

「只有十三盎司，」喜爾福太太回答。「大概就像一顆葡萄柚那麼重。」

「是嘛，這樣子啊，烏龜的成長速度非常緩慢，」荷畢先生一本正經的說。「但是牠們可以活上一百年。」

　　「這個我知道，」喜爾福太太說。「可是我真的好希望牠能夠多長大一點點。牠實在是一個小不點兒。」

　　「可是牠看起來剛好就是牠應該有的樣子。」荷畢先生說。

　　「不，才不呢！」喜爾福太太叫喊著。「想想看，當牠發現自己是如此嬌小時，會是多麼可憐啊！每個人都想要長大。」

　　「妳真的希望牠可以長大一點兒，是嗎？」荷畢先生說，就在他說話的同時，忽然靈光乍現，瘋狂的念頭飛進了他的腦海。

「我當然希望！」喜爾福太太叫道。「我願意付出一切代價來達成願望！對啦，我曾經看過照片裡的烏龜大得人們都可以坐在牠們的背上！萬一阿肥看到牠們，牠會羨慕得臉色發綠吧！」

荷畢先生的心念像個飛輪般飛快轉動著。此時此刻，沒錯，就是他的大好機會！不要錯過了，他告訴自己。千萬不要錯過了！

「喜爾福太太，」他說。「如果妳真的這麼想，我正巧知道怎樣可以讓烏龜長得快點兒。」

「你是說真的嗎？」她大叫。「噢，求求您告訴我！我是不是餵牠吃了不對的東西？」

「我以前曾經在北非工作過，」荷畢先生說。「在英格蘭，所有的烏龜都是從那裡來的，有個游牧的阿拉伯人告訴我這個祕密。」

　　「告訴我！」喜爾福太太叫著。「荷畢先生，我求您告訴我！我願意一輩子都為您做牛做馬。」

　　當他聽到「一輩子都為您做牛做馬」這幾個字，荷畢先生的身體忍不住興奮的顫動。「你等我，」他說。「我得進去寫一些東西給妳。」

　　過了幾分鐘之後，荷畢先生手上拿著一張紙條回到了陽台。「為了怕風把它給吹走，」荷畢先生說，「我要把它綁在繩子上吊下去給妳。下去了喔。」

　　喜爾福太太抓住了紙條，拿到面前。她看到了上面是這樣子寫的：

喂咕嗚，喂咕嗚，點大點大變！

點快，喂咕嗚，生來起，成來起，長來起！

壯茁來起，脹膨來起，大來起！

嚥虎吞狼！食蠶吞鯨！開大口胃！動大指食！

肉肥長，喂咕嗚，肉肥長！

吧來，吧來，吧吃命拼！

「這是什麼意思？」她問。「這是另一種語言嗎？」

「這是烏龜的語言，」荷畢先生說。「烏龜是一種很退縮的生物。因此牠們只了解顛倒著寫的文字。

這是再清楚不過的了，不是嗎？」

「我想是吧！」喜爾福太太迷惑的說著。

「喂咕嗚只不過是把烏龜倒過來念，」荷畢先生說，「妳念看看吧。」

「真的唷！」喜爾福太太說。

「其他的字也都是倒著念的，」荷畢先生說。「如果妳把它們變成人類的語言，簡單的說就是：

烏龜，烏龜，變大點大點！

快點，烏龜，生起來，成起來，長起來！

茁壯起來，膨脹起來，大起來！

狼吞虎嚥！鯨吞蠶食！胃口大開！食指大動！

長肥肉，烏龜，長肥肉！

來吧，來吧，拚命吃吧！」

　　喜爾福太太仔細對照著紙條上的咒語。「我想您說的對，」她說。「太聰明了。不過這裡面有好多的『來起』，它們有什麼特別的意思嗎？」

　　「『來起』在任何語言裡都是很管用的字眼，」荷畢先生說，「尤其是對烏龜而言。喜爾福太太，現在妳需要做的就是，每天早、中、晚三次，把阿肥抱到妳的面前，並且對牠輕輕念著這些話。練習一遍讓我聽聽看。」

喜爾福太太用烏龜話大聲、緩慢的念出了整段話，遇到了奇怪的字眼還會結結巴巴的。

「還不錯，」荷畢先生說。「但是當妳對著阿肥說的時候，要放多一點聲音表情在裡面。我可以拿任何東西跟妳打賭，如果妳做得對，只要幾個月的時間，牠就會比現在大上一倍。」

「我會試試看的，」喜爾福太太說。「任何方法我都會試的。我當然會。但是我不大相信這樣真的行得通。」

「妳就等著瞧吧！」荷畢先生微笑對她說。

　　荷畢先生回到了他的公寓裡之後，全身上下興奮的顫抖著。他不斷重複的喃喃自語，一輩子都為您做牛做馬。真的是好福氣啊！

　　不過在福氣到來之前，還有一大堆的事情得要完成呢。

　在荷畢先生不算大的客廳裡，僅有一張桌子和兩把椅子等簡單家具。他把它們搬進臥房裡去，然後出去買了一大塊厚帆布，並且把它鋪滿整間客廳的地上，好用來保護地毯。

　接著，他拿出電話簿記下了城裡每一家寵物店的地址。一共有十四家寵物店。

他花了兩天的時間，造訪了每一家寵物店，並選購他的烏龜。他打算買很多很多，至少一百隻，也可能更多。而且他必須很小心的挑選。

對你我而言，這一隻烏龜和另一隻烏龜，可能並沒有太大的不同——牠們可能只有大小和外殼的顏色不同。阿肥有著深色的龜殼，所以荷畢先生大肆採購時，只選擇了深色外殼的烏龜。

當然體型大小最要緊。荷畢先生選了各種不同大小的烏龜，有一些只比阿肥的十三盎司大不了多少，有些則是大上了許多，但是他不要任何一隻比阿肥輕的烏龜。

「餵牠們吃甘藍菜葉，」寵物店的老闆告訴他。「牠們吃那個就夠了。還要有一碗水。」

34

　最後，亢奮的荷畢先生已經買了超過一百四十隻的烏龜，他用籃子一次十隻或是十五隻的把牠們帶回家裡。他得走上好幾趟；等全部都運完時，他已經疲憊不堪了，不過這是值得的。好傢伙，真是值得啊！

等到所有的烏龜都一起放進客廳裡面時，那景象真是教人吃驚呀！地板上擠滿了大大小小的烏龜，有一些漫步探險著，有一些嚼著甘藍菜葉，有一些在一個淺淺的大碟子裡喝著水。當牠們在帆布上移動的時候，只會發出非常細微的沙沙聲，沒有別的雜音了。

每當荷畢先生經過客廳的時候，他都得小心找出一條路，踮起腳尖穿過這一片會移動的褐色龜殼海洋。不過已經差不多了。他必須繼續進行別的工作。

　荷畢先生在退休以前是一家巴士維修廠的技工。

現在他回到了以前工作的老地方，問老搭檔可不可以

把他的舊工作？借給他使用一、兩個小時。

　他現在要做的是一件工具，好讓他從陽台上往下

伸到喜爾福太太的陽台上抓起烏龜。這對荷畢先生這樣的技工來說是輕而易舉。

首先他做了兩隻金屬的爪子，之後把它們固定在一根金屬長管的一端。他又在金屬管裡穿進兩條不易彎曲的鐵絲，並把它們接到金屬爪子上。如此一來，當你一拉鐵絲，爪子便夾緊；而當你一推，爪子便會打開來。鐵絲連結到金屬管另一端的把手上面。這一切都再簡單不過了。

荷畢先生準備好要開始了。

喜爾福太太有一份兼差的工作。她每天從正午到下午的五點鐘在一家賣報紙和糖果的店裡工作。而這也帶給荷畢先生許多方便。

第一個令人興奮的午後來臨了，在確認過喜爾福太太出門了之後，荷畢先生便帶著他的金屬長管子走到陽台上——他把這個工具叫作「烏龜捕手」。他斜靠著陽台上的欄杆，將長管子降到喜爾福太太的陽台上。 阿肥正在一旁就著暖和的陽光作日光浴。

「你好啊，阿肥！」荷畢先生說。「你將會有一趟小小的旅程囉。」

他撥弄著烏龜捕手，把它移到了阿肥的正上方，先推開把手讓爪子張得開開的，接著俐落的把兩隻爪子放到阿肥的殼上，再拉起把手。爪子就好像是兩根手指頭一般，緊抓著阿肥的外殼。他把阿肥拉上了他的陽台。真是輕而易舉。

為了確認喜爾福太太說的十三盎司是正確的，荷畢先生把阿肥放到他自己廚房的秤子上。果然沒錯。

現在，他一手捧著阿肥，小心的穿梭在他蒐購來

的烏龜群裡，首先，要找一隻龜殼顏色和阿肥相同的，再來，是要剛剛好重兩盎司的。

　　兩盎司沒有多重。比一顆最小的雞蛋還要輕。不過你知道，重要的是要確認新的烏龜只比阿肥大上一點點而已。差別要小到讓喜爾福太太無法察覺才行。

對荷畢先生來說，要從他的眾多收藏中剛好找到一隻他想要的烏龜，並不是很困難。他想要一隻在他的廚房秤上剛剛好是十五盎司的，不能多也不能少。當他找到時，他把牠放在餐桌上的阿肥旁邊，連他自己也幾乎無法分辨出來哪一隻比較大一點兒。但是牠的確比較大，比阿肥大了兩盎司。這一隻稱為烏龜二號。

荷畢先生將烏龜二號拿到陽台上，用烏龜捕手的爪子抓住牠。然後把牠放到喜爾福太太的陽台

上，正巧把牠放在一顆鮮美可口的萵苣旁邊。

烏龜二號從來都沒有嘗過這麼鮮嫩多汁的萵苣葉——牠向來都只有粗老乾瘦的甘藍菜葉可以吃。牠愛上了萵苣，而且興高采烈的大快朵頤。

接下來是相當緊張的兩個小時的等待——等著喜爾福太太下班回來。

她會發覺這一隻新來的烏龜和阿肥有什麼不同嗎？真是個緊張的時刻呀！

喜爾福太太快步踱到了陽台上。

「阿肥，我的親愛的！」她叫了出來。「媽咪回來了！你有沒有想念我啊？」

荷畢先生小心的躲在兩大株有斑點的盆栽後面，屏住呼吸從他的欄杆後偷偷窺視。

新來的烏龜還在大口大口的吞著萵苣葉。

「天啊，天啊，阿肥，你今天好像真的是餓了，」喜爾福太太說著。「一定是因為我對你念了荷畢先生的神奇咒語。」

荷畢先生看著喜爾福太太拿起了烏龜，並且輕輕撫摸著龜殼。接著，她從口袋裡掏出了荷畢先生的紙條，然後把烏龜拿近她的臉龐，低聲的從紙條上讀出：

喂咕嗚，喂咕嗚，點大點大變！

點快，喂咕嗚，生來起，成來起，長來起！

壯茁來起，脹膨來起，大來起！

嚥虎吞狼！食蠶吞鯨！開大口胃！動大指食！

肉肥長，喂咕嗚，肉肥長！

吧來，吧來，吧吃命拚！

荷畢先生從枝葉叢中探出頭

來喊道：「晚安，喜爾福太太。

阿肥今晚好嗎？」

「噢，牠太可愛了，」

喜爾福太太向上凝視著說。「而且牠的胃口變得好極

了！我從來沒看過牠這樣大吃！一定是因為神奇咒語

的緣故！」

「誰知道啊，」荷畢先生曖昧的說。「誰知道啊！」

荷畢先生足足等了七天才採取下一步行動。

等到了第七天下午，當喜爾福太太去上班時，他把烏龜二號從下面的陽台拉了上來帶進客廳裡。烏龜二號剛剛好重十五盎司。他現在得找一隻恰恰好是十七盎司的烏龜，再多二盎司。

他很輕易就從大量的收藏中找出了一隻十七盎司的烏龜，再一次比對過龜殼的顏色吻合。然後他將烏龜三號放到喜爾福太太的陽台上。

你應該也已經猜到了，荷畢先生的祕密其實很簡單。如果一種生物長得夠慢——我是說真的是非常非常的慢——那麼你將永遠不會發現牠正在長大，尤其是如果你每天都看著牠。

小孩子也是一樣的。他們其實每一個星期都在長高，但是他們的媽媽都得等到他們的衣服穿不下了，才會發覺到。

慢慢來，荷畢先生告訴自己。不要著急。

所以，接下來的八個星期是這樣子的：

一開始是

阿肥 重 13 盎司

第一個禮拜結束時

烏龜二號 重 15 盎司

第二個禮拜結束時

烏龜三號 重 17 盎司

第三個禮拜結束時

烏龜四號 重 19 盎司

第四個禮拜結束時

烏龜五號 重 21 盎司

第五個禮拜結束時

烏龜六號 重 23 盎司

第六個禮拜結束時

烏龜七號 重 25 盎司

第七個禮拜結束時

烏龜八號 重 27 盎司

　　阿肥的重量是十三盎司。烏龜八號是二十七盎司。非常緩慢的，經過了七個星期，喜爾福太太的寵物已經長大，並超過了一倍，而這位傻大姐卻絲毫沒有發現有什麼異樣！

　　即使是對從欄杆向下窺看的荷畢先生來說，烏龜八號看來都是相當的大。在整個計畫進行過程當中，

喜爾福太太幾乎
沒有發現到什麼
不對勁，真是令人
訝異。只有一次，
她向上邊看邊說：「你知道嗎，荷畢先生，我真的覺
得牠長大了一點點，你認為呢？」

　　「我是看不出來有多大不同。」荷畢先生輕鬆的
回答。

不過現在也許已經到了該叫暫停的時候了。有一天傍晚，當荷畢先生正要出去建議喜爾福太太量一量阿肥的體重時，突然間，從樓下陽台傳來一聲嚇人的驚叫聲，一下子就把荷畢先生給吸引了出來。

　　「看！」喜爾福太太大叫。「阿肥大得進不去牠小房子的門了！牠一定長大了很多！」

喂咕嗚愛情咒

「秤秤看吧，」荷畢先生指示她說。「快帶牠進去秤秤看。」

喜爾福太太照著做，半分鐘之後，她雙手高高舉著烏龜在頭上揮舞著走回來，並且呼喊說：「猜猜看怎麼了，荷畢先生！猜猜看怎麼了！牠有二十七盎司重！牠比以前還要重上一倍！噢，親愛的！」她撫摸著烏龜叫道。「噢，你真是個了不起的好小子！瞧一瞧荷畢先生為你做了什麼聰明的事啊！」

荷畢先生突然間變得非常勇敢起來。「喜爾福太太，」他說。「妳想我可以下去妳的陽台，親自抱一抱阿肥嗎？」

「好啊，當然可以！」喜爾福太太說。「立刻下來吧。」

荷畢先生飛奔下樓，喜爾福太太開了門迎接他。他們並肩走出陽台。「好好看看牠！」喜爾福太太說。「牠是不是好了不起！」

「牠現在是個大個兒烏龜了！」荷畢先生說。

「這是拜您之賜！」喜爾福太太叫著，「您創造了奇蹟，真的！」

「但是我要怎麼處理牠的房子呢？」喜爾福太太說。「晚上牠需要有個房子住，但是牠進不去門裡頭。」

他們站在陽台上看著試圖擠進房子裡的烏龜。但是牠太大了。

「我應該要把門弄大一些，」喜爾福太太說。

「別那麼做，」荷畢先生說。「千萬不要劈壞了那麼漂亮的小房子。再說，牠只需要變小那麼一點點兒，很容易就可以進去了。」

「可是牠怎麼變小呢？」喜爾福太太問。

「這簡單，」荷畢先生說。「換一下神奇咒語，不要對牠說變大點變大點，而是告訴牠變小一點點兒。不過當然還是要用烏龜話說。」

「行得通嗎？」

「當然行得通。」

「明白告訴我需要說些什麼吧，荷畢先生。」

荷畢先生拿出了一張紙和一枝鉛筆寫下：

喂咕嗚，喂咕嗚，

點小點小變，點小變。

「這就行了，喜爾福太太，」他把紙條交給她。

「我不介意試試，」喜爾福太太說，「但是你知道，我可不想要牠再度變成一個小不點兒，荷畢先生。」

「牠不會的，親愛的女士，不會的，」荷畢先生說。「只要在今天晚上和明天早上念咒，然後靜觀其變。我們應該會很幸運的。」

「如果行得通的話，」喜爾福太太輕輕碰著他的手臂說，「那麼你就是世上最聰明的人了。」

隔天下午，喜爾福太太一出門上班，荷畢先生立刻把烏龜從她的陽台拉了上來，帶進屋裡。現在他需要做的是去找一隻小一些的烏龜，好讓牠可以剛好穿過那個小房子的門。

　　他挑選出一隻並且用他的烏龜捕手把牠放了下去。接著，他仍然抓著烏龜測試看看牠能不能通過那一扇門。結果牠過不去。

　　他另外又選了一隻，再度測試。這一隻順利的通過了。很好。他把烏龜放在陽台中央一片可口萵苣葉的旁邊，然後回到屋子裡，等待喜爾福太太的歸來。

　　那天傍晚，荷畢先生忽然聽到喜爾福太太興奮顫抖的驚呼聲叫從下頭傳上來，當時他正好在陽台上澆著他的植物。

喂咕嗚愛情咒

「荷畢先生！荷畢先生！您在哪兒？」她大聲叫著。「快來看這個。」

荷畢先生從欄杆上伸出頭來說，「怎麼了？」

「噢，荷畢先生，有效了！」她呼喊著。「您的神奇咒語又對阿肥見效了！牠現在能夠走進牠小房子的門了！真是奇蹟啊！」

「我可以下來看看嗎？」荷畢先生大叫著回應。

「馬上就下來，我親愛的！」喜爾福太太回答他。「下來看看您為了我可愛的阿肥所創造的奇蹟！」

荷畢先生轉身從陽

台跑進客廳，像芭蕾

舞者一般的，用腳尖在擠滿烏

龜的地板上跳躍前進，甩開了他的前門，耳

邊傳來小愛神哼唱著的情歌。他兩步併成一步的

飛奔下樓。這就對了！他低聲告訴自己。我這輩

子最重要的時刻現在即將到來！我不可以亂了方寸！

我不可以沒了分寸！我必須保持冷靜！

　　當他跑下了四分之三的樓梯時，他看見喜爾福太

太已經打開了門，臉上帶著燦爛的微笑在門口準備歡

迎他。她揚起她的雙臂抱住他，大聲歡呼，「您真的

是我所遇過最了不起的人！您真是無所不能！趕快進

來讓我請您喝杯茶以表達我對您微薄的一點心意！」

　　荷畢先生坐在喜爾福太太起居室中舒適的座椅

上，低頭啜飲著茶，渾身興奮又緊張。他望著對面坐著的可愛女士，並對著她微笑。她也微笑回看著他。

她的微笑，是那麼的溫馨與友善，瞬間賜予了他所需要的勇氣，於是他說：「喜爾福太太，妳願意嫁給我嗎？」

「哇，荷畢先生！」她驚呼。「我還以為你不打算要問我呢！我當然願意嫁給你！」

荷畢先生放下他的茶杯，兩個人都站了起來，在房間裡熱情的擁抱。

喂咕嗚愛情咒

「這一切都是阿肥的功勞，」喜爾福太太有點兒喘不過氣的說。

　　「好個老阿肥，」荷畢先生說，「我們會永遠養著他的。」

　　隔天下午，荷畢先生帶著其他所有的烏龜，回到那幾家寵物店去，免費送還給他們。然後把他的客廳打掃乾淨，完全沒有留下一片甘藍菜葉，也見不到一絲養過烏龜的痕跡。

　　幾個禮拜之後，喜爾福太太變成了荷畢太太，他們倆從此過著幸福快樂的日子。

喂咕嗚愛情咒

後記

　　我想你們應該想知道烏龜一號小阿肥後來怎麼樣了。好吧，一個星期之後，牠被一個叫作茹蓓塔‧施貴寶的小女孩從一家寵物店買走了，後來牠就住在茹蓓塔的花園裡。她每天餵牠萵苣、番茄切片和清脆的芹菜，到了冬天牠就在工具房裡裝著乾樹葉的箱子裡頭冬眠。

　　那已經是很久以前的事情了。茹蓓塔現在已經長

大而且結婚了，也有了兩個小孩。她搬家了，不過阿肥還是跟她住在一起，也仍是備受全家疼愛的寵物。茹蓓塔認為阿肥現在應該三十歲了。牠花了那麼長的時間才長到喜爾福太太養牠時的兩倍大小。不過最後牠終於還是長大了。

Author's Note

Some years ago, when my own children were small, we usually kept a tortoise or two in the garden. In those days, a pet tortoise was a common sight crawling about on the family lawn or in the back yard. You could buy them quite cheaply in any pet-shop and they were probably the least troublesome of all childhood pets, and quite harmless.

Tortoises used to be brought into England by the thousand, packed in crates, and they came mostly from North Africa. But not many years ago a law was passed that made it illegal to bring any tortoises into the country. This was not done to protect us. The little tortoise was not a danger to anybody. It was done purely out of kindness to the tortoise itself. You see, the traders who brought them in used to cram hundreds of them tightly into the packing-crates without food or water and in such horrible conditions that a great many of them always died on the sea-journey over. So rather than allow this cruelty to go on, the Government stopped the whole business.

The things you are going to read about in this story all happened in the days when anyone could go out and buy a nice little tortoise from a pet-shop.

ROALD DAHL
Esio Trot

Mr Hoppy lived in a small flat high up in a tall concrete building. He lived alone. He had always been a lonely man and now that he was retired from work he was more lonely than ever.

There were two loves in Mr Hoppy's life. One was the flowers he grew on his balcony. They grew in pots and tubs and baskets, and in summer the little balcony became a riot of colour.

Mr Hoppy's second love was a secret he kept entirely to himself.

The balcony immediately below Mr Hoppy's jutted out[1] a good bit further from the building than his own, so Mr Hoppy always had a fine view of what was going on down there. This balcony belonged to an attractive middle-aged lady called Mrs Silver. Mrs Silver was a widow who also lived alone. And although she didn't know it, it was

she who was the object of Mr Hoppy's secret love. He had

loved her from his balcony for many years, but he was a

very shy man and he had never been able to bring himself

to^2 give her even the smallest hint of his love.

Every morning, Mr Hoppy and Mrs Silver exchanged polite conversation, the one looking down from above, the other looking up, but that was as far as it ever went. The distance between their balconies might not have been more than a few yards, but to Mr Hoppy it seemed like a million miles. He longed to invite Mrs Silver up for a cup of tea and a biscuit, but every time he was about to form the words on his lips, his courage failed him. As I said, he was a very very shy man.

Oh, if only[3], he kept telling himself, if only he could do something tremendous like saving her life or  rescuing her from a gang of armed thugs, if only he could perform some great feat[4] that would make him a hero in her eyes. If only ...

The trouble with Mrs Silver was that she gave all her love to somebody else, and that somebody was a small tortoise called Alfie. Every day, when Mr Hoppy looked over his balcony and saw Mrs Silver whispering endearments to Alfie and stroking his shell, he felt

absurdly jealous. He
wouldn't even have
minded becoming
a tortoise himself if

it meant Mrs Silver stroking his shell each morning and
whispering endearments to him.

Alfie had been with Mrs Silver for years and he
lived on her balcony summer and winter. Planks had been
placed around the sides of the balcony so that Alfie could
walk about without toppling over the edge, and in one
corner there was a little
house into which Alfie
would crawl every
night to keep warm.

When the colder weather came along in November, Mrs Silver would fill Alfie's house with dry hay, and the tortoise would crawl in there and bury himself deep under the hay and go to sleep for months on end without food or water. This is called hibernating.

In early spring, when Alfie felt the warmer weather through his shell, he would wake up and crawl very slowly out of his house on to the balcony. And Mrs Silver would clap her hands with joy and cry out, "Welcome back, my darling one ! Oh, how I have missed you !"

It was at times like these that Mr Hoppy wished more than ever that he could change places with Alfie and become a tortoise.

Now we come to a certain bright morning in May when something happened that changed and indeed electrified[5] Mr Hoppy's life. He was leaning over his balcony-rail watching Mrs Silver serving Alfie his breakfast.

"Here's the heart of the lettuce for you, my lovely," she was saying. "And here's a slice of fresh tomato and a piece of crispy celery."

"Good morning, Mrs Silver," Mr Hoppy said. "Alfie's looking well this morning."

"Isn't he gorgeous!" Mrs Silver said, looking up and beaming at him.

"Absolutely gorgeous," Mr Hoppy said, not

meaning it. And now, as he looked down at Mrs Silver's smiling face gazing up into his own, he thought for the thousandth time how pretty she was, how sweet and gentle and full of kindness, and his heart ached with love.

"I do so wish he would grow a little faster," Mrs Silver was saying. "Every spring, when he wakes up from his winter sleep, I weigh him on the kitchen scales. And do you know that in all the eleven years I've had him he's not gained more than three ounces[6] ! That's almost nothing !"

"What does he weigh now?" Mr Hoppy asked her.

"Just thirteen ounces[7] ," Mrs Silver answered. "About as much as a grapefruit."

"Yes, well, tortoises are very slow growers," Mr Hoppy said solemnly. "But they can live for a hundred years."

"I know that," Mrs Silver said. "But I do so wish he would grow just a little bit bigger. He's such a tiny wee fellow."

"He seems just fine as he is." Mr Hoppy said.

"No, he's not just fine!"

Mrs Silver cried. "Try to think how miserable it must make him feel to be so titchy[8] ! Everyone wants to grow up."

"You really would love him to grow bigger, wouldn't you?" Mr Hoppy said, and even as he said it his mind suddenly went click and an amazing idea came rushing into his head.

"Of course I would!" Mrs Silver cried. "I'd give anything to make it happen! Why, I've seen pictures of giant tortoises that are so huge people can ride on their backs! If Alfie were to see those he'd turn green with envy!"

Mr Hoppy's mind was spinning like a fly-wheel[9]. Here, surely, was his big chance! Grab it, he told himself. Grab it quick!

"Mrs Silver," he said. "I do actually happen to[10] know how to make tortoises grow faster, if that's really what you want."

"You do?" she cried. "Oh, please tell me! Am I feeding him the wrong things?"

"I worked in North Africa once," Mr Hoppy said. "That's where all these tortoises in England come from, and a bedouin[11] tribesman told me the secret."

"Tell me!" cried Mrs Silver. "I beg you to tell me, Mr Hoppy! I'll be your slave for life."

When he heard the words your slave for life, a little shiver of excitement swept through Mr Hoppy. "Wait there," he said. "I'll have to go in and write something down for you."

In a couple of minutes Mr Hoppy was back on the balcony with a sheet of paper in his hand. "I'm going to lower it to you on a bit of string," he said, "or it might blow away. Here it comes."

Mrs Silver caught the paper and held it up in front of her. This is what she read:

ESIO TROT, ESIO TROT,

TEG REGGIB REGGIB!

EMOC NO, ESIO TROT,

WORG PU, FFUP PU, TOOHS PU!

GNIRPS PU, WOLB PU, LLEWS PU!

EGROG! ELZZUG! FFUTS! PLUG!

TUP NO TAF, ESIO TROT, TUP NO TAF!

TEG NO, TEG NO! ELBBOG DOOF!

"What does it mean?" she asked. "Is it another language?"

"It's tortoise language," Mr Hoppy said.

"Tortoises are very backward creatures. Therefore they can only understand words that are written backwards. That's obvious, isn't it?"

"I suppose so," Mrs Silver said, bewildered.

"Esio trot is simply tortoise spelled backwards," Mr Hoppy said. "Look at it."

"So it is." Mrs Silver said.

"The other words are spelled backwards, too," Mr Hoppy said. "If you turn them round into human language, they simply say:

TORTOISE, TORTOISE,

GET BIGGER, BIGGER!

COME ON, TORTOISE,

GROW UP, PUFF UP, SHOOT UP!

SPRING UP, BLOW UP, SWELL UP!

GORGE! GUZZLE! STUFF! GULP!

PUT ON FAT, TORTOISE, PUT ON FAT!

GET ON, GET ON! GOBBLE FOOD!"

Mrs Silver examined the magic words on the paper more closely. "I guess you're right," she said. "How clever. But there's an awful lot of poos in it. Are they something special?"

"Poo is a very strong word in any language," Mr Hoppy said, "especially with tortoises. Now what you have to do, Mrs Silver, is hold Alfie up to your face and whisper these words to him three times a day, morning, noon and night. Let me hear you practise them."

Very slowly and stumbling a little over the strange words, Mrs Silver read the whole message out loud in tortoise language.

"Not bad," Mr Hoppy said. "But try to get a little more expression into it when you say it to Alfie. If you do it properly I'll bet you anything you like that in a few months ' time he'll be twice as big as he is now."

"I'll try it," Mrs Silver said. "I'll try anything. Of course I will. But I can't believe it'll work."

"You wait and see," Mr Hoppy said, smiling at her.

Back in his flat, Mr Hoppy was simply quivering all over with excitement. Your slave for life, he kept repeating to himself. What bliss!

But there was a lot of work to be done before that happened.

The only furniture in Mr Hoppy's small living-room

was a table and two chairs. These he moved into his
bedroom. Then he went out and bought a sheet of thick
canvas and spread it over the entire living-room floor to
protect his carpet.

Next, he got out the telephone-book and wrote down
the address of every pet-shop in the city. There were
fourteen of them altogether.

It took him two days to visit each pet-shop and choose his tortoises. He wanted a great many, at least one hundred, perhaps more. And he had to choose them very carefully.

To you and me there is not much difference between one tortoise and another. They differ only in their size and in the colour of their shells. Alfie had a darkish shell, so Mr Hoppy chose only the darker-shelled tortoises for his great collection.

Size, of course, was everything. Mr Hoppy chose all sorts of different sizes, some weighing only slightly more than Alfie's thirteen ounces, others a great deal more, but he didn't want any that weighed less.

"Feed them cabbage leaves," the pet-shop owners told him. "That's all they'll need. And a bowl of water."

When he had finished, Mr Hoppy, in his enthusiasm, had bought no less than one hundred and forty tortoises and he carried them home in baskets, ten or fifteen at a time. He had to make a lot of trips and he was quite

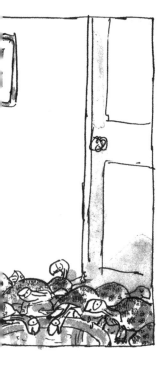

exhausted at the end of it all, but it was worth it. Boy, was it worth it! And what an amazing sight his living-room was when they were all in there together! The floor was swarming with tortoises of different sizes, some walking slowly about and exploring, some munching cabbage leaves, others drinking water from a big shallow dish. They made just the faintest rustling sound as they moved over the canvas sheet, but that was all. Mr Hoppy had to pick his way carefully on his toes between this moving sea of brown shells whenever he walked across the room. But enough of that. He must get on with the job.

Before he retired Mr Hoppy had been a mechanic in a bus-garage. And now he went back to his old place of work and asked his mates if he might use his old bench for an hour or two.

What he had to do now was to make something that would reach down from his own balcony to Mrs Silver's balcony and pick up a tortoise. This was not difficult for a mechanic like Mr Hoppy.

First he made two metal claws or fingers, and these he attached to the end of a long metal tube. He ran two stiff wires down inside the tube and connected them to the metal claws in such a way that when you pulled the wires, the claws closed, and when you pushed them, the claws opened.

The wires were joined to a handle at the other end of the tube. It was all very simple.

Mr Hoppy was ready to begin.

Mrs Silver had a part-time job. She worked from noon until five o'clock every weekday afternoon in a shop that sold newspapers and sweets. That made things a lot easier for Mr Hoppy.

So on that first exciting afternoon, after he had made

sure that Mrs Silver had gone to work, Mr Hoppy went

out on to his balcony armed with his long metal pole. He

called this his tortoise-catcher. He leaned over the

balcony railings and lowered the pole down on to

Mrs Silver's balcony below. Alfie was

basking[12] in the pale sunlight over to

one side.

"Hello, Alfie," Mr Hoppy said. "You are about to go

for a little ride."

He wiggled the tortoise-catcher till it was right above

Alfie. He pushed the hand-lever so that the claws opened

wide. Then he lowered the two claws neatly over Alfie's

shell and pulled the lever. The claws closed tightly over

the shell like two fingers of a hand. He hauled Alfie up on

to his own balcony. It was easy.

Mr Hoppy weighed Alfie on his own kitchen scales just to make sure that Mrs Silver's figure of thirteen ounces was correct. It was.

Now, holding Alfie in one hand, he picked his way carefully through his huge collection of tortoises to find one that first of all had the same colour shell as Alfie's and secondly weighed exactly two ounces more.

Two ounces is not much. It is less than a smallish
hen's egg weighs. But, you see, the important thing in Mr
Hoppy's plan was to make sure that the new tortoise was
bigger than Alfie but only a tiny bit bigger. The difference
had to be so small that Mrs Silver wouldn't notice it.

From his vast collection, it was not difficult for Mr

Hoppy to find just the tortoise he wanted. He wanted one that weighed fifteen ounces exactly on his kitchen scales, no more and no less. When he had got it, he put it on the kitchen table beside Alfie, and even he could hardly tell that one was bigger than the other. But it was bigger. It was bigger by two ounces. This was Tortoise Number 2.

Mr Hoppy took Tortoise Number 2 out on to the

balcony and gripped it in the claws of his tortoise-catcher. Then he lowered it on to Mrs Silver's balcony, right beside a nice fresh lettuce.

Tortoise Number 2 had never eaten tender juicy lettuce leaves before. It had only had thick old cabbage leaves. It loved the lettuce and started chomping[13] away at it with great gusto[14].

There followed a rather nervous two hours' wait for Mrs Silver to return from work.

Would she see any difference between the new tortoise and Alfie? It was going to be a tense moment.

Out on to her balcony swept Mrs Silver.

"Alfie, my darling!" she cried out. "Mummy's back! Have you missed me?"

Mr Hoppy, peering over his railing, but well hidden between two huge potted plants, held his breath.

The new tortoise was still chomping away at the lettuce.

"My my, Alfie, you do seem hungry today," Mrs

Silver was saying. "It must be Mr Hoppy's magic words I've been whispering to you."

Mr Hoppy watched as Mrs Silver picked the tortoise up and stroked his shell. Then she fished Mr Hoppy's piece of paper out of her pocket, and holding the tortoise very close to her face, she whispered, reading from the paper:

"ESIO TROT, ESIO TROT,

TEG REGGIB REGGIB!

EMOC NO, ESIO TROT,

WORG PU, FFUP PU, TOOHS PU!

GNIRPS PU, WOLB PU, LLEWS PU!

EGROG! ELZZUG! FFUTS! PLUG!

TUP NO TAF, ESIO TROT, TUP NO TAF!

TEG NO, TEG NO! ELBBOG DOOF!"

Mr Hoppy popped his head out of the foliage and called out, "Good evening, Mrs Silver. How is Alfie tonight?"

"Oh, he's lovely," Mrs Silver said, looking up and beaming. "And he's developing such an appetite! I've never seen him eat like this before! It must be the magic words."

"You never know," Mr Hoppy said darkly. "You never know."

Mr Hoppy waited seven whole days before he made his next move.

On the afternoon of the seventh day, when Mrs Silver was at work, he lifted Tortoise Number 2 from the balcony below and brought it into his living-room. Number 2 had weighed exactly fifteen ounces. He must now find one that weighed exactly seventeen ounces, two ounces more.

From his enormous collection, he easily found a seventeen-ounce tortoise and once again he made sure the shells matched in colour. Then he lowered Tortoise Number 3 on to Mrs Silver's balcony.

As you will have guessed by now, Mr Hoppy's secret was a very simple one. If a creature grows slowly enough ——I mean very very slowly indeed —— then you'll never notice that it has grown at all, especially if you see it every day.

It's the same with children. They are actually growing taller every week, but their mothers never notice it until they grow out of their clothes.

Slowly does it, Mr Hoppy told himself. Don't hurry it.

So this is how things went over the next eight weeks.

In the beginning

ALFIE weight 13 ounces

End of first week

TORTOISE NO. 2   weight 15 ounces

End of second week

TORTOISE NO. 3   weight 17 ounces

End of third week

TORTOISE NO. 4   weight 19 ounces

End of fourth week

TORTOISE NO. 5   weight 21 ounces

End of fifth week

TORTOISE NO. 6   weight 23 ounces

End of sixth week

TORTOISE NO. 7   weight 25 ounces

End of seventh week

TORTOISE NO. 8   weight 27 ounces

Alfie's weight was thirteen ounces. Tortoise Number 8 was twenty-seven ounces. Very slowly, over seven weeks, Mrs Silver's pet had more than doubled in size and the good lady hadn't noticed a thing.

Even to Mr Hoppy, peering down over his railing, Tortoise Number 8 looked pretty big. It was amazing that Mrs Silver had hardly noticed anything at all during the great operation. Only once had she looked up and said, "You know, Mr Hoppy, I do believe he's getting a bit bigger. What do you think?"

"I can't see a lot of difference myself," Mr Hoppy had answered casually.

But now perhaps it was time to call a halt, and that evening Mr Hoppy was just about to go out and suggest to Mrs Silver that she ought to weigh Alfie when a startled cry from the balcony below brought him outside fast.

"Look!" Mrs Silver was shouting, "Alfie's too big to get through the door of his little house! He must have grown enormously !"

"Weigh him," Mr Hoppy ordered. "Take him in and weigh him quick."

Mrs Silver did just that, and in half a minute she

was back holding the tortoise in both hands and waving

it above her head and shouting, "Guess what, Mr Hoppy!

Guess what! He weighs twenty-seven ounces! He's twice

as big as he was before! Oh, you darling!" she cried,

stroking the tortoise. "Oh, you great big wonderful boy!

Just look what clever Mr Hoppy has done for you!"

Mr Hoppy suddenly felt very brave. "Mrs Silver," he said. "Do you think I could pop down to your balcony and hold Alfie myself?"

"Why, of course you can!" Mrs Silver cried. "Come down at once."

Mr Hoppy rushed down the stairs and Mrs Silver opened the door to him. Together they went out on to the balcony. "Just look at him!" Mrs Silver said proudly. "Isn't he grand!"

"He's a big good-sized tortoise now," Mr Hoppy said.

"And you did it!" Mrs Silver cried. "You're a miracle-man, you are indeed!"

"But what am I going to do about his house?" Mrs Silver said. "He must have a house to go into at night, but now he can't get through the door."

They were standing on the balcony looking at the tortoise, who was trying to push his way into his house. But he was too big.

"I shall have to enlarge the door," Mrs Silver said.

"Don't do that," Mr Hoppy said. "You mustn't go chopping up such a pretty little house. After all, he only needs to be just a tiny bit smaller and he could get in easily."

"How can he possibly get smaller?" Mrs Silver asked.

"That's simple," Mr Hoppy said. "Change the magic words. Instead of telling him to get bigger and bigger, tell him to get a bit smaller. But in tortoise language of course."

"Will that work?"

"Of course it'll work."

"Tell me exactly what I have to say, Mr Hoppy."

Mr Hoppy got out a piece of paper and a pencil and wrote:

ESIO TROT, ESIO TROT,

TEG A TIB RELLAMS, A TIB RELLAMS.

"That'll do it, Mrs Silver," he said, handing her the paper.

"I don't mind trying it," Mrs Silver said. "But look here, I wouldn't want him to get titchy small all over again, Mr Hoppy."

"He won't, dear lady, he won't," Mr Hoppy said. "Say

it only tonight and tomorrow morning and then see what happens. We might be lucky."

"If it works," Mrs Silver said, touching him softly on the arm, "then you are the cleverest man alive."

The next afternoon, as soon as Mrs Silver had gone to work, Mr Hoppy lifted the tortoise up from her balcony and carried it inside. All he had to do now was to find one that was a shade smaller, so that it would just go through the door of the little house.

He chose one and lowered it down with his tortoise-catcher. Then, still gripping the tortoise, he tested it to see if it would go through the door. It wouldn't.

He chose another. Again he tested it. This one went through nicely. Good. He placed the tortoise in the middle of the balcony beside a nice piece of lettuce and went inside to await Mrs Silver's homecoming.

That evening, Mr Hoppy was watering his plants on the balcony when suddenly he heard Mrs Silver's shouts from below, shrill with excitement.

"Mr Hoppy! Mr Hoppy!Where are you?" she was shouting. "Just look at this!"

Mr Hoppy popped his head over the railing and said, "What's up?"

"Oh, Mr Hoppy, it's worked!" she was crying. "Your

magic words have worked again on Alfie! He can now get through the door of his little house ! It's a miracle!"

"Can I come down and look?" Mr Hoppy shouted back.

"Come down at once, my dear man!" Mrs Silver answered. "Come down and see the wonders you have worked upon my darling Alfie!"

Mr Hoppy turned and ran from the balcony into the living-room, jumping on tip-toe like a ballet-dancer between the sea of tortoises that covered the floor. He flung open his front door and flew down the stairs two at a time with the love-songs of a thousand cupids ringing in his ears. This is it! He whispered to himself under his breath[15] . The greatest moment of my life is coming up now! I mustn't bish it. I mustn't bosh[16] it! I must keep very calm! When he was three-quarters way down the stairs he caught sight of Mrs Silver already standing at the open door waiting to welcome him with a huge smile on her face. She flung her arms around him and cried out, "You really are the most wonderful man I've ever met! You can do anything! Come in at once and let me make you a cup of tea. That's the very least you deserve!"

Seated in a comfortable armchair in Mrs Silver's parlour, sipping his tea, Mr Hoppy was all of a twitter[17]. He looked at the lovely lady sitting opposite him and smiled at her. She smiled right back at him.

That smile of hers, so warm and friendly, suddenly gave him the courage he needed, and he said, "Mrs Silver, please will you marry me?"

"Why, Mr Hoppy!" she cried. "I didn't think you'd ever get round to asking me! Of course I'll marry you!"

Mr Hoppy got rid of his teacup and the two of them stood up and embraced warmly in the middle of the room.

"It's all due to Alfie," Mrs Silver said, slightly breathless.

"Good old Alfie," Mr Hoppy said. "We'll keep him for ever."

The next afternoon, Mr Hoppy took all his other tortoises back to the pet-shops and said they could have them for nothing. Then he cleaned up his living-room, leaving not a leaf of cabbage nor a trace of tortoise.

A few weeks later, Mrs Silver became Mrs Hoppy and the two of them lived very happily ever after.

P.S.

I expect you are wondering what happened to little Alfie, the first of them all. Well, he was bought a week later from one of the pet-shops by a small girl called Roberta Squibb, and he settled down in Roberta's garden. Every day she fed him lettuce and tomato slices and crispy celery, and in the winters he hibernated in a box of dried leaves in the tool-shed.

That was a long time ago. Roberta has grown up and

is now married and has two children of her own. She lives in another house, but Alfie is still with her, still the much-loved family pet, and Roberta reckons that by now he must be about thirty years old. It has taken him all that time to grow to twice the size he was when Mrs Silver had him. But he made it in the end.

查單字

1 jut out：突出、伸出。

2 bring oneself to：說服、引誘、引導。

3 if only：如果……的話該有多好。

4 feat：技藝、武藝、英勇事蹟、偉績。

5 electrify：使震驚，給予……強烈的震憾。

6 ounce：盎司（重量單位，**1** 盎司約相當於 **28**.**35** 公克）。

7 thirteen ounces：約 **370** 公克。

8 titchy：極小的（俗語）。

9 fly-wheel：飛輪，是一種可以儲存旋轉動能的一種裝置。

10 happen to ：偶然，碰巧。

11 bedouin：貝多因人（居住敘利亞、阿拉伯等地帶的阿拉伯遊牧人；遊牧的人；流浪者）。

12 bask：取暖、晒太陽。

13 chomp：（指馬）大聲的嚼，同 champ。

14 gusto：趣味、興趣；with gusto 津津有味的。

15 under one's breath：低聲的、小聲的。

16 bosh：胡說八道；愚蠢的舉。

17 all of a twitter：興奮的，緊張的。

羅爾德 · 達爾

出生：1916 年於英國威爾斯地德蘭道夫誕生

學歷：雷普敦聖彼得市德蘭道夫天主教學校

職業：殼牌石油公司東非代表。第二次世界大戰英
　　　國皇家空軍戰鬥機飛行員，空軍武官，作家。

　　達爾自己的小孩還小的時候，他們常會在花園裡養一、兩隻烏龜。這是在英國公布進口烏龜是違法之前很久的事情了。除了身為作家之外，達爾也是一個聰明的發明家，而且他也真的曾經製造過一個故事裡的烏龜捕手——只不過他是為了要避免彎腰時的背痛，利用它來撿起地板上的東西的。

達爾於一九九〇年去世，享年七十四歲。

生活座右銘

我在兩端同時燒著蠟燭

雖然無法明亮終宵。

但是，

啊，我的敵人和朋友們，

它散發出迷人光彩。

你可以到羅爾德・達爾的網站上尋找更
多與他有關的事情：www.roalddahl.com

羅爾德・達爾
不只說精采的故事……

**你知道嗎？本書作者版稅的 10% 會捐給
羅爾德・達爾慈善機構嗎？**

●羅爾達・達爾優良兒童慈善機構（Roald Dahl's Marvellous Children's Charity）：羅爾德・達爾以故事和韻文聞名，但鮮為人知的是，他其實常常幫助罹患重症的兒童。所以現在羅爾達・達爾優良兒童慈善機構秉承他不凡的善行，幫助數以千計罹患神經或血液相關疾病的孩童，以期接近達爾善良的心。此機構也為英國孩童提供護理照料、醫療設備，以及很重要的——娛樂，並透過先驅研究幫助世界各地的孩童。

你願意拿出實際行動來幫助別人嗎？

詳情請看：www.roalddahlcharity.org。

●羅爾德‧達爾博物館暨故事中心（Roald Dahl Museum and Story Centre）：設立於倫敦郊外的白金漢郡大密森頓市，也是羅爾德‧達爾生前居住與寫作的地方。達爾的信件與手稿展示於博物館的中心位置；另外還有兩間展示達爾生平、充滿童趣的展覽室：一間互動式的故事中心，以及他著名的寫作小屋。

國家圖書館出版品預行編目資料

喂咕嗚愛情咒 / 羅爾德‧達爾（Roald Dahl）著；
昆丁‧布雷克（Quentin Blake）繪；顏銘新譯. --
二版 . --台北市：幼獅，2013.08
　　面；　公分. --（故事館；9）
譯自：Esio Trot
ISBN 978-957-574-920-0（平裝）

　873.59　　　　　　　　　　　　102013614

‧故事館009‧

喂咕嗚愛情咒

作　　者＝羅爾德‧達爾（Roald Dahl）
繪　　圖＝昆丁‧布雷克（Quentin Blake）
譯　　者＝顏銘新
出 版 者＝幼獅文化事業股份有限公司
發 行 人＝李鍾桂
總 經 理＝王華金
總 編 輯＝劉淑華
主　　編＝林泊瑜
美術編輯＝游巧鈴
總 公 司＝10045台北市重慶南路1段66-1號3樓
電　　話＝(02)2311-2832
傳　　真＝(02)2311-5368
郵政劃撥＝00033368

門市

‧松江展示中心：10422台北市松江路219號
　電話：(02)2502-5858轉734　傳真：(02)2503-6601
‧苗栗育達店：36143苗栗縣造橋鄉談文村學府路168號（育達商業科技大學內）
　電話：(037)652-191　傳真：(037)652-251

印　　刷＝崇寶彩藝印刷股份有限公司　　　幼獅樂讀網
定　　價＝180元　　　　　　　　　　　　http://www.youth.com.tw
港　　幣＝60元　　　　　　　　　　　　 e-mail:customer@youth.com.tw
二　　版＝2013.08
書　　號＝987215

幼獅文化公司 ／讀者服務卡／

感謝您購買幼獅公司出版的好書！

為提升服務品質與出版更優質的圖書，敬請撥冗填寫後（免貼郵票）擲寄本公司，或傳真（傳真電話02-23115368），我們將參考您的意見、分享您的觀點，出版更多的好書。並不定期提供您相關書訊、活動、特惠專案等。謝謝！

基本資料

姓名：＿＿＿＿＿＿＿＿＿＿＿＿先生／小姐

婚姻狀況：□已婚 □未婚　職業：□學生 □公教 □上班族 □家管 □其他

出生：民國＿＿＿＿年＿＿＿＿月＿＿＿＿日

電話：（公）＿＿＿＿（宅）＿＿＿＿（手機）＿＿＿＿

e-mail：＿＿＿＿＿＿＿＿＿＿＿＿

聯絡地址：＿＿＿＿＿＿＿＿＿＿＿＿

1.您所購買的書名： **喂咕嗚愛情咒**

2.您通常以何種方式購書?：□1.書店買書 □2.網路購書 □3.傳真訂購 □4.郵局劃撥
（可複選）　□5.幼獅門市 □6.團體訂購 □7.其他

3.您是否曾買過幼獅其他出版品：□是，□1.圖書 □2.幼獅文藝 □3.幼獅少年
□否

4.您從何處得知本書訊息：□1.師長介紹 □2.朋友介紹 □3.幼獅少年雜誌
（可複選）　□4.幼獅文藝雜誌 □5.報章雜誌書評介紹＿＿＿＿＿報
□6.DM傳單、海報 □7.書店 □8.廣播(　　　　)
□9.電子報、edm □10.其他＿＿＿＿

5.您喜歡本書的原因：□1.作者 □2.書名 □3.內容 □4.封面設計 □5.其他

6.您不喜歡本書的原因：□1.作者 □2.書名 □3.內容 □4.封面設計 □5.其他

7.您希望得知的出版訊息：□1.青少年讀物 □2.兒童讀物 □3.親子叢書
□4.教師充電系列 □5.其他

8.您覺得本書的價格：□1.偏高 □2.合理 □3.偏低

9.讀完本書後您覺得：□1.很有收穫 □2.有收穫 □3.收穫不多 □4.沒收穫

10.敬請推薦親友，共同加入我們的閱讀計畫，我們將適時寄送相關書訊，以豐富書香與心靈的空間：

(1)姓名＿＿＿＿ e-mail＿＿＿＿ 電話＿＿＿＿
(2)姓名＿＿＿＿ e-mail＿＿＿＿ 電話＿＿＿＿
(3)姓名＿＿＿＿ e-mail＿＿＿＿ 電話＿＿＿＿

11.您對本書或本公司的建議：

廣　告　回　信
台北郵局登記證
台北廣字第942號

請直接投郵　免貼郵票

10045　台北市重慶南路一段66-1號3樓

幼獅文化事業股份有限公司

請沿虛線對折寄回

客服專線：02-23112832分機208　傳真：02-23115368

e-mail：customer@youth.com.tw

幼獅樂讀網http：//www.youth.com.tw